RESCUE RIDERS
Ghost Pony

Peter Clover

Illustrations by Shelagh McNicholas

DEC · 03

HAPPY CHRISTMAS SHELLY

LOVE, PAT AND BILLY.

Hodder Children's Books

A division of Hodder Headline Limited

To Mark, Alison, Charlotte and Daniel

Text copyright © 1998 Peter Clover
Illustrations copyright © 1998 Shelagh McNicholas

First published in Great Britain in 1998
by Hodder Children's Books

This edition published 2000

A Catalogue record for this book is available
from the British Library

ISBN 0 340 72681 4

Typeset by Hewer Text Ltd, Edinburgh
Printed and bound in Great Britain by Guernsey Press

Hodder Children's Books
a division of Hodder Headline Limited
338 Euston Road
London NW1 3BH

One

'Something's definitely going on!' said Hannah.

Charlotte looked puzzled, and blinked hard beneath a quizzical frown.

'What is? What's definitely going on?' She tried to sound interested but was actually more concerned with getting Mandrake's bridle on before he started playing up. If Charlotte didn't slip the bit behind Mandrake's teeth at exactly the right moment he would go on strike and clamp his jaws tight. And when Mandrake did that, you needed a crowbar to get the snaffle in. Or at least a pepper-mint!

'YES!' Charlotte exclaimed in triumph as Mandrake took the bit. She turned her attention back to Hannah, who had long since finished tacking up Flash and was now busy with other thoughts.

'So *what's* definitely going on?' asked Charlotte again.

'It's Miles,' said Hannah. She reached forward to smooth out Flash's creamy mane and give him a good rub behind his ears. Flash was a golden palomino whose coat shone like shot silk in the early morning sunlight. 'Miles is definitely up to something!'

Miles was Hannah's stepbrother. He was sixteen and dead keen to be a newspaper journalist when he left school. He now had a Saturday job, helping out at the offices of the local paper. And he'd already managed to get two small news reports printed. Both pieces had been about Hannah. The first was an account of her heroic rescue ride down a Welsh mountain after an accident on an adventure holiday. And the second was about Hannah and her friends saving the old mill on the downs from burning to the ground.

Miles was always on the lookout for a good scoop. He was always in the background somewhere, snooping about like a shadow.

Hannah explained. 'I've noticed that Miles has been leaving the house really early for the last four days. Much earlier than usual. He always leaves before seven anyway for his newspaper round. But since Monday he's been slipping out before six.'

'How do you know?' said Charlotte. 'And why are you awake at that time, anyway?'

'It's the gravel,' said Hannah. 'Those fat tyres on his new mountain bike make a real noise on the drive. And it's right below my bedroom window, so I hear him crunching past as he leaves. Yes! Miles is definitely up to something!'

'I bet it's that ghost pony,' said Charlotte, matter-of-factly. Then she checked Mandrake's girth.

'Ghost pony! *What* ghost pony?' Hannah couldn't believe her ears. She knew nothing about any ghost pony and was

4

surprised that Charlotte did and hadn't told her.

Charlotte pushed her dark hair back off her forehead and crammed her riding hat down on to her head.

'You know,' she said casually. 'The ghost pony. I'm sure I told you. Or someone else must have.'

'You didn't tell me about any ghost pony,' complained Hannah. 'No one did. I can't believe *you* didn't tell me either. I'm probably the last person in the whole universe to know about it! How could you not tell me?'

'Keep your hair on,' teased Charlotte. 'It's no big deal.' She suddenly felt really embarrassed that she had forgotten to tell her best friend about it. 'It's only a story that's going round, Han.'

'And who told you?'

'I overheard my mum on the phone telling her friend about a strange white pony which has been spotted up on the moors. Only a few people have seen it,' continued Charlotte, 'but they all report the same thing. A thin, ghostly pale pony which suddenly appears from no-where, then disappears back into the mist again before anyone can get a really close look.'

'Wow!' breathed Hannah. 'That's fantastic! And I bet that's exactly what big bruvver Milo is up to. He's out on that moor looking for this phantom pony so that he can write about it for the paper. I can see it now: GHOST PONY HAUNTS MOOR!'

'You'd make a great detective, Han,' laughed Charlotte. 'Sharp as a razor, you are.'

Hannah pulled a face. 'If you're so clever, then tell me why Miles hasn't said anything? Why is he being so secretive? I would have thought that I was the first person he would have confided in.'

'I can't believe you've said that, Han. It's quite obvious. Miles knows exactly what you're like. You'd be begging to tag along. You know you would. You'd cramp his style and spoil it for him.'

'No, I wouldn't!' complained Hannah bitterly. Then, 'Yes, I would,' she admitted honestly. 'But wait till I catch up with him anyway. I shan't beg to go along with him. But I *shall* pester him until he tells me everything he knows about it!'

Charlotte swung herself up into the saddle and laughed. 'Something tells me I'm going to be up on that moor really early tomorrow morning.'

'Earlier than you think!' grinned Hannah.

Two

At the very first opportunity, Hannah gave Miles a good grilling. She caught him just at the right moment, the second he arrived home from school.

Poor Miles hadn't even reached the house when Hannah leaped out of the shrubbery and grabbed his handlebars. Miles's bike ground to a crunching halt.

Hannah stood there with his front wheel clamped between her knees.

'Gotcha!' she grinned menacingly.

'Oh no!' groaned Miles. 'The Spanish Inquisition. I knew it was only a matter of time!'

Miles was so desperate to get away that he told Hannah everything right there and then.

'OK, Hannah. Sorry if I shut you out. But it was something I had to do on my own. I wanted a story for the *Echo* and I didn't want anyone else around spoiling it.'

'Spoil it! How could I spoil it?' complained Hannah. She looked hurt and dejected.

'Be real, Hannah. You would have got overexcited at the first sighting,' said Miles. 'You *know* you would. *If* I saw this ghost pony – which I haven't – I didn't want to scare it off in two seconds flat.'

'I could have helped,' insisted Hannah, but really she knew that Miles was right. He usually was. If she had seen the ghost pony, Hannah would probably have screamed. She would have become so excited that she wouldn't have been able to stop herself.

'Anyway,' continued Miles. 'I've been scouting the moor for days now and I haven't seen a thing. No ghost. No pony. Nothing!'

Hannah jumped in with her own theory.

'Maybe you've not been looking in the right places. Perhaps you should have asked me, after all. I know all about ponies. Even ghost ones,' she added. 'I bet I could have found it. And don't tell me you were out looking on this mountain bike!' Hannah's eyes rolled up to her brows. 'No wonder you haven't seen anything. You need a pony. A real pony to attract a ghost one.'

Hannah had already made up her mind. It was going to be easy. *She* would be the one to solve this mystery of the haunted moor. With a little help, of course, from Charlotte and Jade.

The next day was Friday, so Hannah

decided that they should be up on the moor really early to fit in a good hour's search before school.

Hannah telephoned Charlotte and told her to be ready in the paddock at six.

'*Six!* Are you crazy?'

'We could make it earlier, if you like!' said Hannah.

'Very funny. Like five-fifty-five, you mean?'

'Oh, be a sport, Charlie. It's got to be that early. Miles said there have only been three real sightings, and they were all in the early hours of the morning; between six and seven-thirty.'

'I thought ghosts only came out at night!' queried Charlotte.

'So did I,' said Hannah. 'But apparently this one doesn't. It's an early bird.'

'I thought it was a pony!' joked Charlotte.

'Ha ha ha. Does that mean you'll come, then?' said Hannah. 'I'll even promise to laugh at *all* your crummy jokes if you do!'

'You'd better, Hannah Robinson. Or I'll

torture you and force you to listen to them twice.'

'I'm not *that* desperate, Charlotte Partridge.'

'Yes, you are. See you in the paddock at six.' Then Charlotte hung up and Hannah found herself laughing down the vacant mouthpiece.

She knew she could rely on Charlotte. Now she just had to telephone Jade. Hannah couldn't wait to tell her her plan.

The following morning was crisp and frosty. The sun had barely woken up and, as yet, hadn't gathered enough strength to burn away the misty veil which hung over the Willows.

Charlotte looked half-asleep beneath her riding hat as she sat astride Mandrake with her eyes closed. Hannah mounted alongside, swinging herself lightly on to Flash's back. The air was still. The only sounds were those of jangling bits and the creak of saddle leather.

A small patch of sunlight eked its way through the band of trees which lined the far side of the paddock. Hannah drew in a long, deep breath. The morning smelled good. It was always great riding with the early sun.

'Are you ready?'

Charlotte opened one lazy green eye.

'As ready as I'll ever be,' she muttered. 'This had better be good!'

The two ponies were already alert and wide awake. Ready for anything. Ears pricked, eyes bright, they snorted and sniffed the fresh, dewy air.

Hannah clapped Flash's arched neck and ruffled his creamy mane. 'What ghost pony is going to be able to resist making friends with this beauty!'

Flash really was a stunning pony. A golden palomino with fine features, a long ivory-coloured tail, and a creamy-white mane. He was a direct contrast to the dark majesty and power of Mandrake. Side by side, the ponies made a magnificent pair.

'Walk on,' Charlotte urged Mandrake forward. 'If we don't leave soon, I'm off back to bed!'

She leaned forward wearily and un-hooked the latch on the paddock gate. Hannah followed, and soon the two friends were trotting their ponies down the deserted lane, on their way to the moor.

Three

They cut across two fields behind the Willows and walked up a narrow cart path which flanked the downs and eventually led on to the moor.

The air was sharp with the scent of gorse. And the sky had now brightened, with shafts of sunlight breaking through the distant mist, spotlighting a sea of purple heather.

Hannah filled her lungs and let out a long, contented sigh. 'Smell that, Charlie. There's nothing quite like it, is there? Out on the moor while the rest of the world sleeps!'

Charlotte had to agree. The ride had woken her up and she now felt invigorated, bright and alive.

'It's brill, Han. Even if we don't see this ghost pony, just being out here with Mandrake and Flash is worth the effort.'

They walked on until they reached the flattest part of the moor, then took off at a steady canter to Saxon Rock, where they were meeting Jade.

Jade didn't have a pony. But when Hannah had telephoned her the night before and told her that she was dragging Charlotte out on to the moor on a ghost hunt, Jade wanted to be in on it too.

'I can ride Jurassic out to Saxon Rock,' she'd said. 'Easy-peasy. That's my side of the moor anyway.' Jade lived in a converted mill which bordered the downs.

The moor was only three kilometres from her front door.

'It'll take you hours on that bone-shaker you call a bike!' Hannah told her. 'I thought that model was extinct!'

'Rubbish. I'm really fast. Bet I'm there before you,' Jade had boasted. And she was too!

Jade had been there for at least ten minutes, stashed her fossil of a bike behind the even more ancient landmark and was lying in wait for her two friends.

Jade glanced at her watch and checked the time. Six-thirty precisely. She looked up. Apart from the early patches of mist, Saxon Rock offered a great vantage point across the sweep of moor. Jade passed the time scanning the horizon for a hint or glimpse of the phantom pony. Seeing none she concentrated on the shapes of two riders emerging from a white drifting veil as they trotted clear into a patch of sunlight.

It was Hannah and Charlotte. Who else could it be! Who else would be crazy enough to be up and out on the moor at six-thirty in the morning?

Jade noticed how the sunlight bounced off Flash's mane, making it glare like white silver. His golden coat shone bright and yellow next to Mandrake's black and glossy one, which looked like polished ebony.

Two stunning ponies, thought Jade. Each totally different from the other. Different looks, different personalities. Just like their riders. Jade yearned to have a pony of her own and pondered over the possibility.

If I *did* ever have a pony, thought Jade, I wonder what it would look like? What it would *be* like. Calm and docile or a right nutter? She rather fancied something between Flash and Mandrake in both personality and colour.

'A fancy piebald,' she said aloud. 'Or a strawberry roan. Something red and fiery to match my hair.' It was something Jade often fantasised about. A pony of her very own. Then she wouldn't have to rely on hiring from Mrs Bellow's riding school. *And* she could meet up with her friends to ride the moor at any time she liked.

Although Hannah and Charlotte couldn't see Jade, both Flash and Mandrake sensed that she was there, hiding behind the rock. So, when Jade began moaning and wailing like a ghoul, it was the riders who were startled, not the ponies.

Flash's ears did flatten a *little*. And Mandrake *did* jig a sideways hop. But it was Hannah and Charlotte whose eyeballs nearly dropped from their sockets.

Hannah had been miles away, indulging herself in daydreams of ghostly gallopings and races with phantom ponies across the moor. And Charlotte was busy thinking of all the toast and marmalade she was going to demolish when she got back home. Neither of them were prepared for Jade's sudden appearance.

'Told you I'd get here first!' shouted Jade, as she leaped out into view.

Hannah and Charlotte could have killed her. But then it was typical of Jade to stage such an entrance.

'How long have you been here, you idiot?' This came from Charlotte.

'Oh, ages. At *least* three hours!'

'Only three! And have you seen anything yet?' Hannah grinned, waiting for a reply.

Jade shrugged her shoulders. 'Nope, nothing.'

'Perhaps it's been and gone. Maybe we got here too late!' said Hannah.

'Too late! It's not even seven o'clock yet,' cried Charlotte.

'Come on, then,' said Hannah. 'Let's not waste any more time. Hop up behind me, Jade, and we'll go further out on to the moor. It looks mistier out there. More like ghost country.'

Four

The three girls spent a good hour patrolling the area where the ghost pony had been seen.

'Miles said that all three sightings were from people out exercising their dogs,' announced Hannah. 'All on different days, but at similar times. And each report described the sound of drumming hooves, then a ghostly pony appearing out of the mist before disappearing again without trace.'

'There was also a rumour about an eerie whinny echoing across the moor long after the ghost pony has gone,' added Charlotte. 'Apparently it's a sound that freezes your bones.'

Hannah shivered at the thought. It was enough to make your blood curdle. 'No wonder Miles has been investigating this mystery,' she said. 'It's really spooky. It would make a fantastic story for the *Echo*.'

But after patrolling for at least one hour and seeing nothing unusual at all, the 'ghostbusters' became a little dispirited. That was when they swore that if there really was a ghost pony haunting the moor, then no one else was going to see it again before them.

They swore a pact and exchanged high fives, which was a little bit difficult for Hannah, who had to twist round on Flash to clap palms with Jade.

Jade was giggling so much that she began to slide off Flash's rump. She tightened her grip around Hannah's waist to steady herself, but then her foot caught Hannah's and knocked her boot clean out of the stirrup iron.

They both slipped to the left and it was only a combination of joint willpower which prevented them from falling. That, and a hefty shove from Charlotte.

Safely positioned once more in the saddle, Jade, riding tandem, couldn't resist a poke to Hannah's ribs.

But it wasn't the unexpected jab which made Hannah gasp. With all the larking around, they'd momentarily forgotten all about their ghost pony. Now it was standing directly in front of them, staring with wild, bulging eyes. Its ears flattened against its low hung head as it observed the trio with interest.

Hannah spoke first in a hushed whisper. Despite everyone previously predicting that she would scream with excitement, Hannah remained cool and calm, even though her heart was thumping against her ribs.

'It's looking straight at me!' Hannah's eyes fastened like magnets upon the ghost pony's face. 'It's so pale and thin,' she said. 'It *can't* be a ghost, can it? It looks so real.'

Jade was clinging to Hannah like ivy, craning her neck for a better view.

Charlotte's mouth formed an oval of disbelief. None of them could believe what they were seeing. Even Flash and Mandrake looked startled.

White mist swirled at the ghost pony's feet, making it difficult to tell where the fog ended and the pony began. They both seemed to be as one.

'It looks half-starved,' said Jade. 'See how its ribs show through its coat. And look how thin its legs are.'

'That's one hungry ghost,' added Charlotte.

'I don't think it *is*,' said Hannah. 'I mean I don't think it's a ghost at all. It looks too real.'

'It *is* real, Han,' agreed Jade. 'It looks half-dead but it's real all right. I'm certain of it.'

Both Flash and Mandrake were very curious. Flash extended his head and took in the unfamiliar scent of the new pony. Mandrake blew a soft snort and shook his head, jangling his reins, eager to step forward and greet the strange newcomer.

But the phantom pony was having none of it. Suddenly, as though a spell had been broken, it turned heel and fled, disappearing back into the mist on thundering hooves. As quickly as it had appeared, it was gone, leaving the girls yearning to see it again.

'Wow!' breathed Hannah, finally. 'I was hoping, really hoping, but I never honestly expected to see it on our first expedition. That was fantastic! We saw it. We actually, *really* saw it!'

'Brill!' exclaimed Charlotte. 'But it looked so sad. Did you see its face? The poor thing looked so starved.'

'I can't believe it either,' uttered Jade. 'It looked so wild. Where did it come from?'

'And where has it gone?' said Hannah.

'It's obviously made its home around here somewhere. It must have,' said Charlotte. 'But *where* is something we'll have to find out.'

'This mist is too thick,' said Hannah. 'And we've got school. We can't possibly go looking now.'

'We've got to come back tomorrow,' urged Jade. 'Or later!'

'Can't tonight,' said Charlotte. 'There's the match, remember?'

'Well, luckily it's Saturday tomorrow,' said Jade. 'We'll be able to come out all over the weekend and search this moor from end to end, top to bottom.'

'We'll find this pony if it's the last thing we do,' said Hannah. 'Agreed?'

Charlotte and Jade nodded. They all felt the same. There was a real pony out here somewhere that needed their help. And soon.

Five

None of the girls could really sleep that night, they were so excited. Getting up the next morning at five-thirty came as a relief.

Jade was on her bike, Jurassic, and away before sunup – about the same time as Hannah and Charlotte were tacking up their ponies.

Charlotte was on a real high and hurrying Hannah to get a move on.

'Come on! Come on! It might be out there waiting.' Charlotte could hardly contain herself.

'Have you got the pony nuts?' asked Hannah.

'Both pockets full,' grinned Charlotte.

'Mine too! And the hay?' Charlotte held up the plastic carrier she was holding.

They jostled their ponies through the gate and made their way up the lane at a fast trot.

By the time they edged on to the moor, their canter had almost broken into a gallop.

Jade watched their approach, standing on the top of Saxon Rock with her flame-coloured hair frizzing out behind her in the morning breeze.

Luckily, there was quite a squall blowing and it was keeping the mist off the moor.

Jade swung up on to Flash and settled herself neatly behind Hannah. Everyone was eager to get going. Even Flash and Mandrake seemed to sense that something was about to happen.

The sun broke through and was trying really hard to be on form at such an early hour.

'It looks different today!' said Jade. 'Is this the same spot where we saw it yesterday?'

'Give or take ten metres,' said Charlotte, 'this is *exactly* the same spot!'

A short distance in front of them, a thin copse of trees sprung up out of the heather. The trees made a natural screen, hiding a shallow basin which sloped down behind on to a narrow track.

The remains of a low dry-stone wall appeared at the end of the track some distance away and formed itself around what looked like the wreck of an old allotment garden. A rough pathway led from the garden to a second thicket of trees, behind which lay the ruins of an old crofter's cottage. If you didn't know it was there, you would never have thought of looking for it. The cottage was completely hidden from view on this lower, flatter section of moor.

'A secret hideaway,' breathed Hannah.

'Just perfect for a frightened pony,' said Charlotte.

'I wonder why Miles didn't find it?' said Hannah.

'Probably concealed by the mist,' suggested Jade. 'It's been pretty thick these past few days.'

The ruined cottage was no more than a few broken walls. The roof was missing, long since collapsed under the passage of time. But a freshwater brook still trickled past its door, which must have once served the crofters who lived on this deserted part of the moor.

They stopped on the ridge at the second thicket of trees and looked down at the cottage, surveying the layout.

'I bet it's down there!' said Hannah. 'I bet that's where it's been hiding, the poor thing. Living off the moor.'

'It *would* be an ideal place,' agreed Jade.

'A perfect place,' said Charlotte. 'Come on, let's tether the ponies and go down on foot. If we ride down we might scare it off again.'

'If it *is* down there,' said Hannah. 'We're only assuming, after all!'

Charlotte raised an eyebrow and gave Hannah a special look as though she knew what they were going to find. They all hoped the ghost pony would be down there but none of them wanted to raise their hopes.

'Come on, then,' said Jade. 'Nice and easy. Only whispers from now on.'

They tied Flash and Mandrake to a low branch and crept on foot towards the cottage ruins. Hannah put her hand in her pocket and felt for the pony nuts. She was hoping to tempt the ghost pony with the offer of a tasty snack.

They approached with caution. Jade found herself holding her breath and had to be reminded to breathe normally.

At any minute, they expected the ghost pony to burst from its hiding-place and go charging past with its wild mane flying and its crazy eyes staring like a creature possessed.

But it didn't do either. It wasn't there.

They walked round the cottage walls feeling totally disappointed. The place was deserted. No sign of a pony anywhere.

The three girls looked at each other. Hannah shrugged her shoulders. 'I was almost certain of it.' Her voice tailed off. Now she was staring past the cottage at a broken, twisted barn, held together with ivy, only ten metres away. She raised her arm slowly and pointed.

'Look! There.' She managed to catch her breath and whisper softly. 'I can see something. Over there. It's the pony. Look!'

Charlotte and Jade narrowed their eyes. And, sure enough, peering out through a gap in the barn's wooden slats, was the ghost pony.

They could just make out the pale white shape of its head amongst the dappled patches of shadow cast across the barn.

Hannah's heart began to pound with excitement. They had found what they were looking for.

The ghost pony was aware of their

presence and shifted its feet restlessly. Behind them, Flash called with a shrill whinny and Hannah answered back over her shoulder. 'It's all right, boy. I haven't forgotten you.' Hannah's hand closed around the pony nuts in her pocket.

She walked on ahead, making soft cooing noises, holding the treats at arm's length.

The ghost pony suddenly came alive. A lovely grey head swept up. Eyes nervous, ears pricked in anticipation, it watched Hannah approach.

It's going to be easy, thought Hannah. She only had to stretch out her hand and the ghost pony would be eating gently from her palm. If only she could just gain its confidence.

Then, suddenly, a look of fear swept across the pony's face. It reared up and swung around, then hurtled out of the barn as though its life depended on it. The poor thing was obviously terrified.

It was impossible to stop the pony without being trampled. All the girls

could do was watch, as it careered away in a wild charge, crashing through the thicket on to the path and the moor beyond.

Mandrake started as the ghost pony thundered past, bucking and kicking in its wake. And Flash threw up his head and blew a worried snort as the phantom steed galloped by.

'Sorry,' said Hannah. 'I wasn't quite quick enough, was I? Mind you, I don't think I could have held it anyway. Did you see the way it reared up?'

'It seemed really frightened,' said Charlotte.

'But at least we've seen it again,' said Jade, 'and now we definitely know that it's real.'

'*Very* real,' said Hannah. 'It even had its registration number freezemarked on to its withers. I just caught a glimpse of it as he hurtled past.'

Jade turned to the others. 'I wonder what it's doing up here all on its own?'

'Somebody's dumped it,' said Charlotte. 'Turned it out on to the moor and left it to fend for itself.'

'Do you really think so?' said Jade. 'If that's true, then it's not doing a very good job for itself, is it? The poor thing looked more like a skeleton than a pony.'

'We've got to catch it,' said Hannah. 'We've just got to!'

Charlotte and Jade didn't need to say anything. Their faces told exactly how they both felt.

Hannah scooped the pony nuts from her pocket and piled them on a flat stone. 'I'll leave these here, just in case it comes back.'

Charlotte did the same and scattered the hay. Between them, they made a nice little picnic to tempt their elusive phantom.

'We'll come again tomorrow nice and early,' said Charlotte, finally. 'Only, this time we'll bring a head collar and lead rein.'

Six

At home, Hannah kept their discovery a secret. She didn't tell Miles what had happened, even when he'd asked cheerfully if they'd had any luck.

Hannah simply shrugged her shoulders and said they were going out again even earlier the following morning.

'But you'll be the first to know when

there's something definite to report,' she added. 'It'll be *your* scoop, Miles. You'll be the first one we tell, promise!'

Hannah grinned, and Miles looked quizzical. He wasn't stupid. He knew Hannah wasn't telling him everything.

The truth was this: Hannah felt really excited about finding the ghost pony and she didn't want to spoil things halfway through. She didn't want Miles taking over. Hannah could understand now why Miles hadn't told her when *he* wanted to do his own thing. She wanted to take things nice and easy. And, above all, Hannah and her friends wanted to be the ones who brought the ghost pony safely off the moor.

The next day was Sunday. Sundays normally meant lazy mornings of doing nothing. Just waiting for lunch, with the smell of Sunday roast wafting across to the paddock field. Then afternoons, for grooming, larking around and a gentle ride. But this Sunday was different.

Hannah leaped out of bed at five-thirty, eyes bright, wide awake and eager to get going.

Unbelievably, Charlotte was already in the paddock, with Mandrake champing at the bit.

'I've been here all night,' she laughed. 'Couldn't sleep.' She had even tacked up Flash. All Hannah had to do was grab the bag of feed and launch herself into the saddle.

Charlotte waved a lead rope and head collar.

'Thought these might come in handy,' she said. 'We're going to need something to lead it off the moor with, aren't we?'

Hannah nodded. Then a thought suddenly struck her. What were they actually going to *do* with this stray pony once they had caught it?

It was only after they met up with Jade that the answer seemed absolutely clear.

*

'I was up half the night clearing out the stable,' said Jade. 'It's been used as a woodshed for years, but it's a proper stable with a loose box and everything. I've shifted all the logs out into the shed and given it a good sweep and hose-down. It will be perfect for Phantom.'

'Phantom!' exclaimed Hannah and Charlotte together.

Jade's face turned as red as her hair. She held her bottom lip between her teeth and lowered her eyes with embarrassment.

'I hope you both don't mind, but I thought . . .' Her voice trailed off.

'Well . . .' said Hannah and Charlotte together, 'what *did* you think?'

'I thought it would be nice, *if* we caught the pony, that I could give him a home. And that maybe we could call him Phantom.'

'That's brilliant,' said Hannah.

'Excellent,' echoed Charlotte. 'Phantom's a nice name, but do you think you'll be able to keep him? Will your parents be OK with that?'

'Oh, they're already fine,' said Jade. 'Now that I've cleared the stable, they both feel it needs a pony to complete the picture!'

'They're fab, your mum and dad, aren't they?' said Hannah. 'They're really great.'

'So what do you think? You don't mind then?' said Jade. ' – If I call the pony Phantom?'

Hannah and Charlotte both grinned.

'Mind! How could we possibly mind! Phantom sounds *perfect*!'

As the sun settled itself above the moor, ragged clouds parted company to let it shine through. Again, a low mist swirled, hugging patches of gorse and heather, giving atmosphere to the bleak moor.

The three girls smiled at each other. Everything was settled. All that was left was to catch Phantom. And today was the day. They were certain of it!

Once out on the moor, the three girls suddenly felt apprehensive. They were so desperate to catch Phantom and start his rehabilitation.

They rode out to the ruined cottage, which they now knew Phantom used as a hideaway. Shielded by the half-grown trees, they walked to the narrow path from the thicket on foot, leaving Flash and Mandrake comfortably tethered.

Suddenly, Hannah whispered, 'Phantom,' and all three girls stopped in their tracks. They peered down through the tangled growth of branches in front of the old barn, and there, standing pale and proud, was their pony.

Jade's heart pounded with excitement, thudding in her chest as though it were about to burst. She now knew that, not only had they found their ghost pony, but that they were definitely taking it home.

Jade felt in her pocket and pulled out a handful of pony nuts. Calling softly all the time, they approached Phantom.

Jade went first. She held out the feed and watched intently as the beautiful grey head raised itself to monitor their

approach. Charlotte handed Hannah the head collar.

Phantom pricked up his ears but stood motionless like a marbled statue as they came closer.

'Let me!' urged Jade. 'Please!' She gently took the head collar from Hannah and edged her way towards the pony. Nearer and nearer she crept and still Phantom didn't spook.

'Hello, boy!' Jade's voice was soft and steady. 'Easy now. Easy!' She offered her outstretched palm. Jade was only centimetres away now. 'Easy, boy. Easy!' Jade's palm made contact with the soft velvet muzzle. Phantom's warm breath stirred in Jade's hand. He took the feed.

Feeling calm and in control, Jade slipped on the head collar. She couldn't believe how easy it was. Hannah came forward with more offerings of pony nuts. And Charlotte strode up purposefully to clap Phantom's neck, hard and solid, to show the pony that he was among friends.

Phantom offered no resistance. He seemed to know that, whatever his past held, it was now behind him. Phantom's future lay ahead with these three girls – Hannah, Charlotte and Jade.

Nothing more was said. Everything else happened by instinct. They tipped the feed on to the ground and let the pony have his fill.

Then Jade led Phantom out of the cottage ruins and calmly walked him up to the moor. There was no struggle, no resistance.

Phantom was more than willing to go.

Hannah and Charlotte mounted quickly. Jade swung up behind Hannah and led Phantom on a short rein off the moor and across the downs, heading for Mill House.

By eight o'clock that Sunday morning, Phantom was stabled and tearing sweet fodder from his hay net.

A clean stable. A roof over his head and a sense of belonging. What more could an abandoned pony want?

Seven

The next day, school seemed to go on forever. Double maths lasted an eternity. It seemed like weeks before the home bell sounded. And Hannah, Charlotte and Jade couldn't get away quick enough.

Three bikes sped along Westway, heading for Mill House, on the downs. Three bikes with three intrepid riders, pedalling like fury to meet their rescued charge – Phantom the ghost pony.

The dappled grey seemed perfectly well at home. Jade's parents said that he had been as good as gold all day.

'Not a peep out of him,' smiled Jade's mother. 'He's a beautiful pony. Wonderful temperament. I can't think what he was doing out on the moor like that, all on his own!'

'Abandoned,' said Mr Falmer. 'Just left to fend for himself, poor fellow. Some people have no heart. They want locking up. Phantom's a wonderful pony. He deserves a good home!'

'So, can I *definitely* keep him, then?' said Jade.

'Of course you can,' said Mrs Falmer. 'As long as he's not sick.'

'He's skinny,' said Hannah.

'That's different,' smiled Jade's father. 'Skinny's not sick. Skinny we can cope with.'

'We'll get the vet over later to take a look at him,' said Mrs Falmer.

Jade listened to her parents and felt all warm and cosy inside. It was obvious that they were as taken with Phantom as Hannah, Charlotte and herself. It was like a dream come true. At last, Jade had a pony of her own!

But for how long? Jade had noticed registration numbers freeze-marked on to Phantom's withers. That meant that he actually belonged to someone. Even if that someone *had* abandoned him on the moor.

Jade knew that, before she could really call Phantom her own, she had to track down the owner and solve the mystery that surrounded him.

It was something she didn't want to think about, but something she *had* to do.

It was Wednesday before Jade found the number of the registry office. Secretly, she was deliberately not trying very hard to obtain it. Hannah had suggested the Yellow Pages, but it was Charlie who came up with the obvious answer.

'Why don't we just ask Mrs Bellows? She's bound to know.'

Mrs Bellows knew everything there was to know about ponies. She simply looked up the number in her Filofax and scribbled it down on the back of an envelope.

'Let me know how it goes,' said Mrs Bellows.

But Jade didn't want to let anyone know anything. She wanted to forget all about Phantom's freeze mark. She didn't really want there to be a registered owner. Jade wanted Phantom to belong to *her*, without any complications. Phantom looked happy in his stable. He'd settled down so quickly in his new home and had already lost that spooked, haunted look. And, although he was very thin and bony, the vet had given him a clean bill of health.

Miles had already started writing his story and now he offered to telephone the number for Jade and make the necessary inquiries. Miles was good on the phone. He sounded so grown up. And, if there were any problems, then Miles would be just the person to handle them.

Jade gave him the envelope with the number on and Miles made the call.

It turned out that Phantom was really called Chevron Blue and registered to a Mr Alfred C. Pollock in Lapswood, a small village on the other side of the moor.

At first, Jade thought that it would be best if she wrote a letter to Mr Pollock. But Charlotte seemed to think that letters would take too long.

'This Mr Pollock might not answer straight away,' said Charlotte. 'He might not even answer at all, especially if he *did* deliberately turn Phantom out on to the moor. If he didn't want Phantom, then he probably doesn't want anyone to know about it either. After all, it's illegal, isn't it? Abandoning a pony?'

'But what if Phantom has simply escaped?' said Hannah. 'Gone missing from his stable or, worse, been stolen and managed to get away? What should we do then?'

'Well, we've got a name and address, haven't we?' said Charlotte. 'Why don't we just ride over there. Check it out, do a recce, have a little snoop around. Ask a few questions. Find out what this

Mr Alfred C. Pollock is like. If Phantom's lost, missing or been stolen, then someone is bound to know about it!'

They all agreed and thought that going over there was a great idea. Partly because it meant that they didn't have to admit to anyone just yet that they actually *had* Phantom. And partly because they were really curious about what someone who could abandon a pony would look like.

'Beady eyes and a thin mouth with no lips,' said Hannah.

'No! I bet he's fat and bald with a greasy moustache,' added Jade.

Before Charlotte could add her impression, Phantom poked his head over the stable door and nuzzled the back of her neck. Charlotte stroked his face and pressed her cheek against the gentle pony.

'*You* know what he looks like, don't you, boy? I bet he's really horrible. A nasty piece of work.' Phantom blew a gentle whicker. He seemed to be in total agreement.

That same day, after tea, the three friends rode over to Lapswood. Jade hired a pony from Mrs Bellows and joined Hannah and Charlotte on the edge of the downs.

Lapswood was only a forty-minute ride away across the moor so they were there in no time at all.

Lapswood was a small village. More of a hamlet really. A simple scattering of cottages and a handful of shops. The combined post office and general store seemed the most likely place to begin their inquiries.

Hannah slipped lightly from the saddle and went inside. Charlotte held Flash and exchanged a raised eyebrow with Jade. Flash pricked up his ears and wondered where Hannah was going as she disappeared into the shop.

Hannah edged up to the counter and picked up a chocolate bar.

'That'll be twenty-four pence,' said the bored, middle-aged shopkeeper. She eyed Hannah with a curious suspicion, as though she didn't often see strangers in Lapswood.

As Hannah paid for the chocolate bar, she made polite conversation.

'I've never been here in Lapswood before,' she began, 'and I only live across the moor.'

'Would that be Champton, then?' asked the shopkeeper. 'Some nice houses in Champton.'

'We live on the Willows,' said Hannah. 'Do you know it?'

'Can't say I do.'

But she knew the answer to Hannah's next question.

'Do you know of a Mr Pollock who lives here in Lapswood?'

'Alf Pollock,' said the shopkeeper. 'Oh, yes. Everyone knows Alf Pollock. Lives up the lane in that monstrosity called Starhanger. Small man, very flash. Nothing of him really. Thin pencil tache.' She would have been happy to go into more detail – she and Mr Pollock were obviously *not* friends. But Hannah had all the information she needed. She made her excuses and left the shop. She couldn't wait to tell the others!

Eight

Starhanger was easy to find, just like the shopkeeper had said. It was a new house, built like a castle, with turrets, crenellations and towers. It was awful. The whole thing was painted a pale, sickly pink.

'Whoever lives here,' said Hannah, 'must be just as sickly and awful.'

'I can't believe anyone would build a house like that!' gawped Jade.

'They have, though, haven't they?' said Charlotte. 'And here comes our Mr Alfred C. Pollock right now, if I'm not mistaken.'

A rather thin man, who looked a bit like a monkey, sauntered down the drive of the pink house. Although it was quite warm, Mr Pollock wore a sheepskin coat with a huge fur collar and matching gloves.

He also had a thin greasy moustache like Jade had predicted.

The three girls sat on their ponies at the foot of the drive and tried to look casual, as though they were just passing. Flash and Pickles were calm and stood motionless, but Mandrake was restless, and pawed at the ground as Mr Pollock approached.

The small, thin man looked up at Mandrake and openly admired Charlotte's pony.

'He's a beauty, isn't he? Black Beauty, just like in the book.'

Charlotte grinned. She thought that was a really oily thing to say. Or maybe it was just the way he said it! She immediately made up her mind that she didn't like this man. And neither did Mandrake. Come to that, neither did Hannah and Flash or Jade and Pickles. All the ponies and riders, for some unknown reason, took an instant dislike to Mr Pollock.

'That palomino's a stunner too!' he continued. Then he shot a glance at Jade and Pickles. 'Pity about yours, though,' he said. 'Reminds me of a pony I had once. Useless, it was. Not like these two. No doubt *they'd* both fetch a good price at auction.'

The girls looked horrified. This man obviously looked at ponies and only saw money. He judged them by how much he thought they were worth. Jade grabbed at the opportunity to probe further.

'What kind of a pony was it?' she asked. 'The one you had? The useless one. What colour was it? How big?'

'Fourteen hands. Grey. Light dapple on its hindquarters. Only got it for my darling Clarissa because she liked the colour. Matched a jacket she'd just bought. Then she went off it, just like that. Not the jacket – the pony. Too nervy for her to ride anyway. Picky eater, too. Cost me a fortune to stable, so I got rid of it.'

This is easy, thought Jade. Mr Pollock certainly liked to talk about himself. She never expected to get so much information out of him so quickly.

'So who did you sell it to?' continued Hannah. 'Was it someone local?'

Suddenly, Mr Pollock went very quiet and looked shifty. Charlotte immediately sensed that he was about to clam up and hurry along on his way. She acted quickly and beamed him her biggest smile.

'We're only interested because a friend of ours has found a pony on the moor. Pale grey, fourteen hands. People say it was turned out, abandoned. But *we* thought that it must have escaped from somewhere!'

Mr Pollock eyed Charlotte suspiciously but he stayed to listen as she continued.

'This friend of ours has always wanted a pony, so she's looking after this one she's

found until she can trace its owner.'

'Why does she want to trace the owner?' snappped Mr Pollock.

'Well, as it's illegal to turn a pony out on to a moor . . .' began Hannah.

'Illegal!' echoed Mr Pollock.

'Yes, illegal,' said Hannah. 'So naturally we thought that the pony must have escaped from somewhere.'

'And we thought that the owner might be frantically worried!' This was Jade joining in.

By now the girls knew for certain that Phantom had been deliberately abandoned, and were enjoying every minute of watching Mr Alfred C. Pollock squirm. After all, *he* had no idea that the girls knew who he was.

Mr Pollock pulled up his fur collar and bobbed his head left and right, checking up and down the length of the road. His voice turned to a hushed whisper.

'I happen to know on good authority—' Here, Mr Pollock tapped the side of his nose '—that the pony you're obviously talking about *was* turned out. It was abandoned because its owners had fallen on hard times and couldn't afford to keep it. Tell your friend from me that she should forget all about tracing any so-called owners and just think herself lucky that she's got a pony of her own at last. No point in stirring up trouble if she's got what she wants, is there?' And, with that, Mr Pollock turned on his heels and hurried away up the road.

As soon as he disappeared around the first corner, the girls screamed 'Yes!' and three fists punched the air.

'You heard what he said! Straight from the horse's mouth,' joked Charlotte.

'I can keep him! That's what he said, isn't it? Phantom's mine. I can keep him. I've actually got a pony. I can't believe it!' Jade had never felt so happy.

'That *was* him, though, wasn't it?' said Hannah. 'That *was* Alfred C. Pollock? We *did* question the right man?'

'Fits his description like a sheepskin glove,' said Charlotte. 'You worry too much, Han.'

Nine

Jade couldn't believe that her dream had come true. The small, rough-looking stable next to the studio workshop shone like a new pin. And, over the next few weeks, Phantom fattened out nicely. Rounded out and muscled, with a healthy sheen to his coat, Phantom gleamed in the early evening sunlight. His grey coat was so light, it almost seemed to glow. He was a calmer pony now, and adjusted to his new home.

Phantom stood cropping grass in the treeless, open section of the orchard, which Mrs Falmer had planted to the side of Mill House. The view beyond opened out across the downs, sweeping away to a carpet of rolling green and mottled heather.

Sitting on the stone-built wall containing the new orchard, Jade watched Phantom.

She admired his long white tail swishing with contentment, and noticed how his fine, silver mane almost touched the ground when he grazed. He was putting on weight, but his ribs still protruded a little.

Another week and you'll be perfect, thought Jade.

Suddenly, Phantom became aware of Jade. He raised his fine head, then gave a loud whinny and trotted over towards her with his high, flowing gait.

Phantom stopped at the wall and pushed his soft muzzle into Jade's hand. Jade felt a lump in her throat and swallowed hard.

She thought she was the luckiest girl alive.

'Whoop, whoop, heeey you!' The tranquil peace was shattered by a familiar war cry. The drumming of hooves reached Phantom's ears. He recognised the sound instantly, and threw up his head to take in the scent of Flash and Mandrake as they galloped across the downs with their riders.

Phantom had only been with Jade for a short time, but already he was a changed pony. The wild, crazy look had been replaced by a calm, trusting gaze. No longer timid and shy with Flash and Mandrake, Phantom looked forward to their visits.

Jade had wanted to pack some meat on to Phantom's bones before she tried him with a saddle. But the vet had told her he'd fill out steadily. 'Don't rush things by any means, but do get a saddle on him. He wants to be ridden.' Those were his very words and they had stuck in Jade's mind.

Jade wasn't quite sure how Phantom would react, but she needn't have worried. Phantom was brilliant. A good, solid ride. Sometimes a little skittish when out on the vast expanse of downs, but that was where Flash and Mandrake came in. Phantom felt reassured with the two ponies alongside and his panic settled. He was coming along brilliantly.

It was time for a ride now. Phantom whickered softly and pranced on the spot, eager to greet his new friends.

Jade slid off the wall. Phantom's saddle hung over the gate and his bridle nestled in the crook of her arm.

Jade was really keen to go riding. This evening, Charlotte was going to give her some pointers.

Although Jade was an excellent rider, Charlotte had a knack of noticing things about ponies and their funny ways. Charlotte could be a little blunt at times but she really knew her stuff. Sometimes, it takes someone else to stand back and look at the whole picture. And this was Charlotte's speciality.

Jade wanted Phantom to be the best, so she didn't mind a lecture from Charlotte.

She pressed her riding hat down on to her frizzing mass of copper-coloured hair and quickly tacked up.

Out on the downs, under Charlotte's instruction, Jade rode Phantom in wide circles at a sitting trot.

'Change to a walk,' called Charlotte, 'then walk to trot, trot to walk and halt!'

Jade did everything Charlotte said, then listened carefully, nodded her head and bit her tongue to stop herself arguing as Charlotte went on.

'Lighten your aids, Jade. You're too heavy with him. I know he *was* skin and bone, but he almost looks like a thoroughbred now. I'm sure he'll respond to a whisper if you give him the chance! Just the slightest touch.'

'Go easy, Charlie,' said Hannah with a grimace.

'Don't be so soft, Han. You want to know, don't you, Jade?' called Charlotte. 'And we need to work on balancing your seat as well! Phantom is probably the lightest ride you'll ever know!'

It was all true. Jade knew that Charlotte was absolutely right. Phantom was so responsive to the lightest aids. Anything heavy made him uncomfortable and confused. Then he became flighty.

Riding Phantom was like breathing air. He was an absolute delight and as different from Flash and Mandrake as Jade was from Hannah and Charlotte. Phantom's power lay in his swift agility and lightness on the hoof.

The ride back home across the downs was ace. Jade couldn't believe that only three weeks ago she didn't even know Phantom existed. And now she couldn't imagine ever being without him.

On her father's suggestion, Jade had written to Mr Alfred C. Pollock informing him that she had found Phantom out on the moor and was willing to keep him and look after him as her own. It was a formality to show that she had made every effort to trace the owner. It didn't mean much to Jade because Mr Pollock had already admitted that he didn't want Phantom any more. But it made Jade's parents happier all the same. At the very least it proved that Jade was honest and responsible.

Funnily enough, Jade hadn't given it another thought once she had posted the letter. The possibility of ever seeing Mr Pollock again had never even crossed her mind. Which was why Jade suddenly felt her stomach turn to lead and her heart bang against her ribs when she saw him standing by his flashy car outside Mill House on their return.

'What's *he* doing here?' gasped Jade.

What bothered Jade most was that Mr Pollock was about to find out that *she* was Phantom's new owner and not the make-believe friend they had invented when they spoke to him three weeks ago. Jade was uncertain as to how he would react to their little deception. It shouldn't matter, though, thought Jade. Mr Pollock had made it quite clear that he didn't want Phantom any more. So what was he doing waiting at Mill House?

Ten

Hannah and Charlotte rode up alongside in a tight formation. They both sensed that Jade was worried sick.

'I wonder what he wants,' said Charlotte.

'Perhaps he's come with Phantom's papers or something,' suggested Hannah. 'You know, to make Phantom really yours, legally.'

Jade hoped so, but her instincts and the butterflies churning her insides told her differently.

The three girls rode up to the entrance of the drive. Overhead, dark ragged clouds had gathered, turning the sky black, like a dark omen.

When Phantom saw Mr Pollock, he reared up and gave a shrill whinny. Jade had to force her seat down hard to stay in the saddle and shorten Phantom's reins to calm him down.

'Woahh, boy. Steady.' She clapped Phantom's neck as he skipped sideways, spooked by the man's presence.

'Bag of nerves,' said Mr Pollock loudly. 'Always was. Always will be. Can't think why this friend of yours wants to keep him.' He stared at Jade with a knowing look, then glanced up the drive to the house. It looked really impressive, especially since the repairs and the new paint job after the fire.

'Or is it really *you* that wants Chevron

Blue?' Mr Pollock directed his cold, beady eyes back to Jade.

Jade felt her face burning red. She felt that she wanted to scream but spoke quietly and calmly.

'I'm sorry, Mr Pollock,' she said, 'that we didn't ask you outright about Phan . . . Chevron Blue the other week. It seemed easier to pretend that Phan . . . Chevron Blue was being looked after by another friend. I so much wanted to be able to keep him!'

'Well, you've done a good job of fattening him out, I must say. Still a bit bony, mind you. But then he always *was* picky over his food. Would never touch his grass cuttings.'

'Grass cuttings!' Jade's mouth hung open in disbelief.

Mr Pollock eyed Phantom up and down. 'Mmmm,' he said. 'Expect he'll fetch a couple of hundred now, though!'

'What do you mean?' Jade sounded horrified. 'I'm not going to sell him! Not ever!!'

'No. *You're* not,' sneered Mr Pollock, 'but *I* am. To the abattoir. He's worth at least two hundred and fifty of their money, I'm certain of it.'

'You can't!' snapped Charlotte. She sounded so angry. 'You gave him away to Jade. He's not yours to sell any more.'

Mr Pollock laughed. He waved a big envelope in his hand and said, 'I've got papers in here that say quite differently. And, as you already know, it's *my* name on the registration form. So there's nothing you can do about it, is there? Unless, of course, you've got two hundred and fifty pounds?'

Jade's jaw dropped open. All three girls were gobsmacked.

'I'm glad I didn't post this now,' said Mr Pollock. He tucked the envelope deep into his pocket. 'I'd driven over to give you these papers. You were that near to keeping him.'

'Now, calm down, Jade! Sit here and tell me all about it.' Mrs Falmer made Jade

sit at the kitchen table and tell her everything in detail. Jade couldn't stop shak-
ing.

'And where is this Mr Pollock now?'
she asked.

'He's gone. Says he'll be back tomorrow
for Phantom. He's going to take him
away, Mum. Take him away and sell
him to the abattoir for horsemeat!'

Mum's brows knitted themselves into a
tight furrow. She looked both angry and
concerned at the same time.

'And you say he wants two hundred and fifty pounds?'

Jade's bottom lip began to tremble. Hannah draped an arm across Jade's shoulder and gave her a hug.

'He couldn't get rid of Phantom quick enough before, could he? Now, when he's starting to look fit and healthy, suddenly he wants him back.'

'But only so that he can sell him,' said Charlotte. 'Mr Pollock doesn't *really* want Phantom. All he wants is two hundred and fifty pounds.'

'Well, there we are then,' said Mrs Falmer. 'No problem. If Mr Pollock wants two hundred and fifty pounds for Phantom then we'll pay him. Things are a bit tight at the moment but I'm sure we can manage that, Jade. Now stop worrying. It's over. We'll pay Mr Pollock what he wants and sort all this out in the morning.'

It sounded too simple to be true. And indeed it was.

*

The next day things got worse. Jade's father telephoned Mr Pollock to tell him they would buy Phantom. But Mr Pollock suddenly doubled the price on Phantom's head and demanded five hundred pounds.

'Five hundred pounds!' said Mr Falmer. He couldn't believe it. 'That's daylight robbery.'

'It's the price,' replied Mr Pollock smugly. 'It's what I've been offered at the abattoir and it's what I want.'

'I think the police might be interested in this,' said Mr Falmer. 'Did you know it's against the law to abandon a pony on public land? I think you could find yourself in real trouble.'

'Go on, Dad. You tell him,' whispered Jade.

But Mr Pollock just laughed down the telephone. 'You've got to prove that though, haven't you?' he said. 'And, as far as I'm concerned, Chevron Blue escaped from his stable and has been living rough on the moor. I've a letter here from your daughter saying that she found him there, so I'd be very careful of what you say if I were you, or the price might suddenly go up again. But I'll tell you what. I'll give you a whole week to raise the money. That's seven whole days. And, as a special bonus, tell that daughter of yours that she can keep Phantom, or whatever it is she calls him, until then, at no extra cost. Seven days. I'll be in touch!' Then he hung up the telephone and the line went dead.

Eleven

Later that day, after school, the girls had a meeting over at Hannah's house. Heads were being put together and fund-raising plans were being made. One in particular.

It was Miles's idea really. He had suggested that he could change the ghost pony story he had written for the *Echo* and turn it into a plea for local donations to help save Phantom's life. He had started rewriting his article straight away and was now working flat out to have it typed up and ready for publication in Tuesday's edition, the following day.

Jade followed Hannah and Charlotte out to the paddock. Flash, Mandrake and Phantom were quietly cropping the grass as the sky turned pink overhead with the setting sun.

'Don't worry, Jade,' said Hannah. 'We'll raise the extra money somehow. I'm sure Miles's article will stir a response.'

'But it's such a lot of money!' fretted Jade.

'Well, I've got some savings in the post office,' added Hannah. 'It's not much, but it's yours!'

'So have I,' offered Charlotte. 'And I could sell my portable CD player – I hardly ever use it!'

'No, you won't,' said Jade. 'It's very kind of you but if anyone is going to sell their things then it will be me! Phantom means more to me than anything. And, if it comes to the worst and we can't raise the money, then I'd sooner release him back on to the moor than hand him over to that rat Pollock!'

Hannah gave Jade a hug. 'It won't come to that. No one's going to take Phantom away from you. Everything will be all right, you'll see!'

'That's exactly what Miles said. But I can't help having my doubts.'

'Then let's just keep our fingers crossed,' said Charlotte, 'and hope that donations start coming in when Miles's article is published tomorrow!'

'And don't forget – we've got seven days. Anything can happen in a week,' said Hannah, reassuringly.

Jade wished that she could share Charlotte and Hannah's enthusiasm. In fact, *everyone* except Jade seemed to be looking on the bright side. Everyone was hopeful, but all Jade could do was look at Phantom and feel her heart painfully breaking. She couldn't help it. She just felt so sad.

Only when Jade was riding Phantom did her spirits lift a little. Smoothing Phantom's arched neck with her hand and running her fingers through his fine, silky mane gave her such a warm feeling. Phantom still had a long way to go before he was in tiptop condition, but he had improved no end. His legs looked sturdier. His shoulders and rump were rounder and his tummy no longer tucked up. His pale-grey, almost white coat gleamed silver, and his eyes shone;

healthy, bright and alive. He responded to Jade's faintest whisper and her lightest aids. Jade hardly needed to move in the saddle any more. Only her hands, light and sensitive on the reins, were needed to influence and control the pony's gait and direction.

That evening at Mill House, Jade had a long talk with her mother.

'I know you're struggling with money,' said Jade, 'and that you can't really afford the two hundred and fifty pounds anyway. But I'm so desperate to keep him. There must be *something* we can do!'

It was true, money *was* scarce. The renovations to Mill House were taking every spare penny. And the fire in the studio had destroyed some of the pieces Mrs Falmer was hoping to sell at the gallery auction the coming Saturday.

But then Jade's mother had an idea. It had been puzzling her as to where she had seen Mr Pollock before. She had only caught a brief glimpse of him from the house, but something about him was familiar! Suddenly, she knew what it was. She'd often seen that flashy car outside the gallery. Mr Pollock had collected his wife from the gallery in it several times when she had been there looking at paintings. Clarissa Pollock liked art and fine things. Especially big, bright, gaudy pictures. She always chose the biggest, brightest paintings on display. So Mrs Falmer decided to paint a picture especially for Clarissa Pollock. A painting that she wouldn't be able to resist. But she didn't tell Jade about her plan. She just said 'Don't worry, Jade, we'll find the money somehow,' and gave her daughter a reassuring cuddle.

It took two days before there was any response from Miles's appeal. Then donations started flooding in. They were only small sums at first, but it seemed that the readers of the *Echo* were more than willing to donate any spare cash they had to help save a pony's life.

Phantom seemed to sense that something was going on. It was almost as though he knew that he was about to be taken away from his new home.

He became even more docile and affectionate towards Jade. He nuzzled up to her at every opportunity and would stand motionless with his head snuggled into Jade's chest as she petted and stroked his handsome face. And if Jade left him for more than a few moments he would become restless and paw the stable floor, scraping the flagstones noisily with his hoof until she returned to reassure him that everything was all right.

Hannah and Charlotte were very enthusiastic about the donations, as the total grew each day, but somehow Jade couldn't raise her spirits to meet theirs. All she could think of was losing Phantom to the abattoir for a measly five hundred pounds.

After school, at every opportunity, Jade took Phantom out with Flash and

Mandrake. Jade thought Hannah and Charlotte were lucky. No one was going to take *their* ponies away.

As the week sped by, Phantom gained more weight and looked the picture of health. At least he'll have more of a chance of survival out on the moor if I *do* release him, thought Jade.

She didn't want to, but she was prepared to do it. She could take his feed out to him, and keep a saddle and bridle at the ruined cottage. Jade preferred these secret thoughts to the prospect of his death at the abattoir. How could he possibly be sold for horsemeat when he was such a beautiful pony? It made Jade feel sick just thinking about it.

Meanwhile, in the privacy of the Mill House studio, Mrs Falmer worked night and day on her painting.

She worked fast in acrylics. The painting was big, bright and bold. Clarissa Pollock would love it.

Mrs Falmer hadn't told Jade about her plan. She didn't want to tell her until the painting was finished. There was an exhibition and sale of work by auction on Saturday, the day of Mr Pollock's deadline to raise five hundred pounds. Jade's mother had already spoken to Mr Allbright, the gallery owner, and arranged for the painting to be included.

By Friday evening, Miles reported that ninety pounds had been donated in response to his article.

'Ninety pounds is a lot of money,' said Jade, 'but it's nowhere near what we need. Even with the two hundred and fifty that Mum and Dad have promised, that still leaves one hundred and sixty pounds to find.' It seemed hopeless.

Jade sat at the kitchen table at Mill House with Hannah and Charlotte. No one was saying anything. Jade looked crestfallen; close to tears. Not at all like the bright cheerful girl they knew. And Mrs Falmer couldn't mention the painting in case it all went wrong.

At last the painting was finished. The auction was taking place in the morning. All Jade's mum needed was an accomplice. Someone who sounded good on the telephone. Someone who could pretend he was an art buyer and convince Mr Allbright that he was bidding for a rich client by phone. Suddenly, she thought of Miles. He would be perfect!

Twelve

Later that afternoon, Mrs Falmer announced that she had to pop out for a while. She took the Range Rover and drove over to the Willows. She called in on Miles and told him of her plan. Miles was very keen to help and Mrs Falmer began coaching him straight away. She went over the drill again and again until Miles was word-perfect.

The following morning, Jade's mother sneaked out with the painting and delivered it to the gallery.

She had telephoned Mrs Pollock the day before and had pretended to be Mr Allbright's assistant.

'There's a wonderful painting in the auction tomorrow that you simply *must* see!' she had said. 'I'm only telephoning because you are a regular client and I *know* that this is a painting you *must* have!'

That was all that was needed to arouse Clarissa's interest.

At nine-thirty, Saturday morning, Clarissa asked Mr Pollock to drive her to the gallery. He dropped her off, then went back to Lapswood to collect a horse box.

At ten o'clock, Jade tacked up Phantom for the last time. She had already decided that today she was going to release Phantom back on to the moor. Jade now realised that, even with the donations from the *Echo*, there wasn't going to be enough money to pay Mr Pollock. Jade was going to lose her pony. At least, out on the moor, Phantom would stand a fighting chance.

Jade had told Hannah and Charlotte the night before of her intentions. And both girls couldn't help but agree that perhaps releasing Phantom was the best solution.

They arranged to meet up at Saxon Rock at eleven o'clock. Mr Pollock had already telephoned that morning and said that he would be coming over at twelve noon. Either to collect the money or to collect Phantom.

Well, he's going to be in for a big surprise, thought Jade. If Mr Alfred C. Pollock wants Phantom, then he's going to have to catch him.

Meanwhile, at the gallery, things were well under way. Clarissa Pollock had seen Mrs Falmer's painting and decided that she just *had* to have it.

By coincidence, at exactly the same time that the girls met at Saxon Rock, lot number five at the gallery came up for sale.

'A contemporary masterpiece,' announced the auctioneer. 'Acrylic on canvas, entitled "Rhapsody in Pink" – an explosion of colour! May I start the bidding at fifty pounds?'

Clarissa Pollock raised her catalogue and bid.

'I have fifty pounds,' said the auctioneer. 'Do I hear seventy-five? Yes! A telephone bid for seventy-five pounds. Do I hear one hundred?'

Clarissa raised her catalogue and bid.

'One hundred,' said the auctioneer. 'Do I hear one hundred and twenty-five? A telephone bid. Yes. Do I hear one hundred and fifty?'

The plan was working brilliantly. All they needed was to raise one hundred and fifty pounds. Mrs Falmer crossed her fingers behind her back. Miles was raising the price of the painting as his telephone performance went according to plan. But would it work?

Clarissa blew out a long sigh and raised her catalogue.

'One hundred and fifty pounds!'

'Yes!' In her mind, Jade's mother punched the air. But she hardly dared to move. She stood calm, trying to suppress the grin rising within her.

She waited for the auctioneer to close the bidding. *They had done it!* They had raised the money!

Then, suddenly, Mrs Falmer couldn't believe her ears.

'I have a telephone bid,' the auctioneer continued. 'One hundred and seventy-five pounds. Do I hear two hundred?'

Jade's mother gasped. 'What on earth is Miles doing? He's messing the whole thing up!'

'Do I hear two hundred?' asked the auctioneer. The gallery fell silent. All eyes were on Clarissa Pollock. She shook her head.

'Telephone bid for two hundred pounds, going once . . .'

Mrs Falmer's stomach turned a violent somersault.

'. . . going twice . . .'

They were in deep trouble now.

'Two hundred pounds!' yelled Clarissa.

Mrs Falmer blew out a sigh of relief and Miles hung up the telephone. He couldn't believe he had let himself get so carried away.

Leaping down the stairs two at a time, Miles grabbed the appeal money from the kitchen mantle and flew out of the house to meet Jade's mother.

Mr Falmer was standing outside in the orchard just as Hannah and Charlotte came riding up across the downs on Flash and Mandrake. He was surprised to see that Jade was up on Flash, seated behind Hannah.

'Where's Phantom?' he asked. 'What's happened to him?'

At first Jade looked sheepish. Then she slipped off Flash and blurted out the truth. 'I *was* going to say that Phantom had run off. But he hasn't. I let him go,' she said. 'There was no way that I could hand him over to be sold for horsemeat, so I've released him back on to the moor. I know you're going to be cross, but I've done it and I'm not sorry!'

Mr Falmer looked at Jade and smiled. What she had done was typical of Jade.

'I'm not cross,' he said. 'I understand. In fact I don't blame you at all. But you know you can't do that, Jade, don't you? It's not right! And Mr Pollock will be here shortly. You'll have to go back and fetch him.'

Jade looked up at Hannah and Charlotte. She didn't want to disobey her father, but she didn't want to go and bring Phantom back either.

But it didn't look like she was going to have to. The two girls were staring past Jade, their eyes fixed on something behind her.

Jade spun round. 'Oh, no! Phantom!' The grey pony was trotting purposefully towards them. He'd followed them home. Jade was so choked with emotion that at first she didn't notice the horse box trundling up the rough road to Mill House.

It was only when he pulled up outside the entrance that Jade registered that Mr Pollock had arrived to collect Phantom.

But as Mr Pollock jumped out of the horse box, Phantom saw him, turned on the hoof and bolted back out across the downs.

'Oi! That's my pony,' yelled Mr Pollock. 'You've just let him go. I saw you with my own eyes!'

Just then, Miles and Mrs Falmer arrived in the Range Rover. 'What's all this fuss about?' said Jade's mum, climbing out from the driver's side.

'*She's* just let my pony go,' complained Mr Pollock. 'It's gone galloping off across the downs!'

'Well, that's exactly what *you* did when you decided to get rid of him, isn't it?' snapped Mrs Falmer. She had obviously had enough of Mr Pollock.

'Anyway,' she continued, 'he's not *your* pony any more. Five hundred pounds, you said. Here!' She thrust an envelope at Mr Pollock. 'Take it. It's all there. And I'll have the registration papers, please!'

Mr Pollock reached inside his jacket and handed over the papers.

'And I'd like a signature on these, right now!' insisted Jade's mother, waving them in his face.

Mr Pollock decided to sign quickly, before anyone changed their mind about the money.

As he climbed back into the horse box, they heard his mobile phone ringing.

'*How* much?' he almost yelled down the receiver. 'No, of course I don't mind, Clarissa, darling. I'm sure it's a wonderful painting.'

'Oh, Mum! That's brilliant!' said Jade. Then she threw herself at her mother and locked her in a bear hug.

'Phantom's mine! At last, he's really mine. I can't believe it! And no one can ever take him away from me, *ever*.'

'Well, you'd better go and fetch him, then!' laughed Mrs Falmer. 'His stable's empty and waiting.'

Hannah held out her hand and helped Jade swing up behind her into Flash's saddle. The others watched as the two ponies stormed off in a cloud of dust across the downs to fetch the precious phantom pony once more.

'Why didn't you tell me what you were up to?' asked Mr Falmer. 'I could have helped!'

'You might have stopped me!' smiled his wife. 'Anyway, I didn't need any more help. I had Miles and he was brilliant!'

'Almost too brilliant,' said Miles. His face blushed scarlet. 'I got a bit carried away, didn't I?'

'But it all turned out fine in the end,' said Mrs Falmer. 'And did you see Jade's face when she realised that Phantom was finally hers?' said Miles. 'It was a picture!'

'Yes,' said Mrs Falmer, 'and I can't wait until she gets back to see it again.'

But when Jade *did* come back, her face was not a happy one. It was red and puffy where she had been crying. Jade ran into her mother's arms and began sobbing.

'We couldn't find him, Mum! We looked everywhere but we couldn't find him. Phantom's gone! He really *has* gone!'

Thirteen

It seemed unbelievable. After everything that had happened. After raising the money. After paying Mr Pollock. After everything – Phantom had vanished.

'He started off as a ghost pony,' said Jade, 'and now he's disappeared just like one.'

Jade's mother tried to calm her down. She hugged her close and smoothed her hair.

'He's out there somewhere, Jade! We know he is. He can't have gone that far!'

'But he has,' sobbed Jade. 'He's gone. The moor goes on forever. We'll never find him. Phantom's gone!'

It was useless. There was nothing anyone could say. Jade was convinced that Phantom had gone for ever and no one could persuade her differently.

That evening, Jade wouldn't eat anything for supper. All she could think about was Phantom. Where was he? What was he doing? Was he safe?

Hannah and Charlotte already decided to get up at the crack of dawn and patrol the moor, until midnight if necessary, to find Phantom for their friend.

Jade chatted to both of them on the telephone before she went to bed. It was nice to know that she had friends who cared.

But there was a long night ahead and daybreak seemed an age away.

Jade finally fell asleep thinking of ghostly gallops, with phantom ponies cantering through her dreams.

The next morning, Jade woke with a terrific headache. Her body felt numb from the neck down.

As she opened her eyes, Jade saw her mum and dad standing at the foot of her bed.

Both of them were grinning. They had a look about them as though they knew something that Jade didn't.

Jade lay with her head on the pillow, her mane of copper-coloured hair bathed in a square of sunlight which shone through the curtains.

For some reason Jade felt really happy. She didn't understand why. After everything that had happened she would have expected to wake up miserable. But, apart from the headache, Jade just felt overwhelmed.

When she saw her mum and dad, Jade sat up in bed. Her head thumped.

'What are you two looking so pleased about?' asked Jade.

They didn't need to answer. They didn't need to say anything. They just smiled.

Suddenly her headache vanished. Jade flew out of bed and hurried down the stairs.

Out in the stable, Phantom stood with his head resting over the half-door. He saw Jade and blew a soft whicker.

Jade's face collapsed in a flood of tears as she buried her head in his fine, silky mane.

'Oh, Phantom! You came back!' Jade threw her arms around the pony's neck. Phantom had found his way home. Home where he belonged. And Jade knew that she would never, ever, lose sight of him again.

ORDER FORM
Peter Clover

HERCULES

0 340 75268 8	1. New Pup on the Block	£3.50	❏
0 340 75295 5	2. Operation Snowsearch	£3.50	❏
0 340 75294 7	3. Treasure Hound	£3.50	❏

RESCUE RIDERS

0 340 72679 2	1. Race Against Time	£3.50	❏
0 340 72680 6	2. Fire Alert	£3.50	❏
0 340 72681 4	3. Ghost Pony	£3.50	❏

All Hodder Children's books are available at your local bookshop or newsagent, or can be ordered direct from the publisher. Just tick the titles you would like and complete the details below. Prices and availability are subject to change without prior notice.

Please enclose a cheque or postal order made payable to *Bookpoint Ltd*, and send to: Hodder Children's Books, 39 Milton Park, Abingdon, OXON OX14 4TD, UK
Email Address: orders@bookpoint.co.uk

If you would prefer to pay by credit card, our call centre team would be delighted to take your order by telephone. Our direct line *01235 400414* (lines open 9.00am-6.00pm Monday to Saturday, 24 hour message answering service). Alternatively you can send a fax on *01235 400454*.

TITLE		FIRST NAME		SURNAME	

ADDRESS	

DAYTIME TEL:		POSTCODE	

If you would prefer to pay by credit card, please complete:
Please debit my Visa/ Access/Diner's Card/American Express (delete as applicable) card no:

Signature...Expiry Date.....................................

If you would NOT like to receive further information on our products please tick the box. ❏